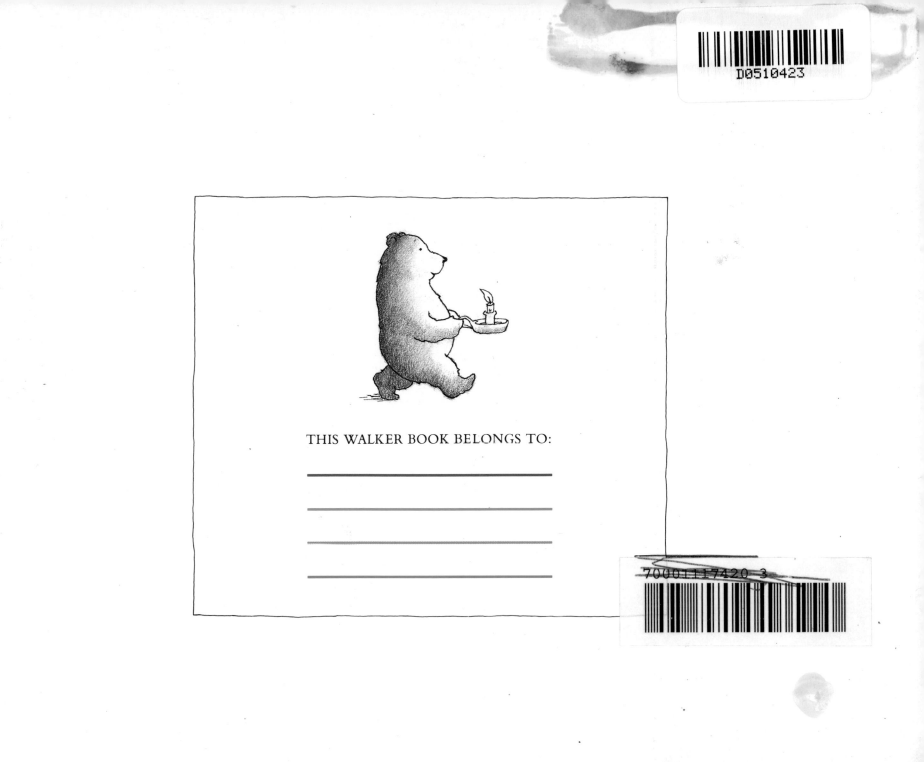

THIS WALKER BOOK BELONGS TO:

_____

_____

_____

_____

For Matthew, Charlie, Jack and Sally

First published 1993 by Walker Books Ltd
87 Vauxhall Walk, London SE11 5HJ

This edition published 1994

2 4 6 8 10 9 7 5 3 1

© 1993 Catherine and Laurence Anholt

This book has been typeset in Bembo.

Printed in Hong Kong

British Library Cataloguing in Publication Data
A catalogue record for this book is
available from the British Library.

ISBN 0-7445-3617-0

Here come the
BABIES

Catherine and Laurence Anholt

WALKER BOOKS
LONDON

Here come the babies!

Babies in boxes, babies in boots, babies on backs

Babies in socks, babies in suits, babies in sacks

Babies everywhere!

Babies in coats, babies in cribs, babies with cats

Babies in boats, babies in bibs, babies with bats

What are babies like?

Babies kick and babies crawl,

Slide their potties down the hall.

Babies smile and babies yell,

This one has a funny smell.

What do babies look like?

Wriggles and dribbles and sticking out ears,

Little round faces with rivers of tears.

Babies wear suits which are long at the toes,

They stick out in the middle and up at the nose.

What are mornings like?

Mum and Dad are fast asleep
And all the house is quiet.
I slip into baby's room
And start a little riot.

What are mealtimes like?

Baby throwing tantrums,
Baby throwing fits,
Baby throwing dinner
In little baby bits.

What do babies play with?

Bobbles and bows,

fingers and toes,

Shoes and hats,

sleeping cats,

Frizzy hair,

saggy bear,

Empty box,

Daddy's socks.

What do babies dream of?

Pat-a-cake, pat-a-cake, dickory dock,
Wee Willie Winkie, it's past eight o'clock.

Hey diddle diddle and Little Bo-peep,
Bye Baby Bunting is counting sheep.

What's in a pram?

nappy bag

favourite rag

food to cook

picture book

floppy bunny

something funny

one shoe

baby too

What are two babies like?

Twins, twins,
Alike as two pins,
Double the trouble…

But double the grins!

What is bathtime like?

Babies in a bubble bath,
Building with the bubbles,

Bubbly beards and bubbly hair
And great big bubbly puddles.

What does a baby do?

hug

hold

hide

sleep

smile

slide

jumble

juggle

jump

bang

burp

bump

totter

tumble

throw

gurgle

giggle

grow

What do lots of babies do?

One baby bouncing on her brother's knee,

Two in a play-pen, three by the sea,

Four babies yelling while their
mummies try to talk,

Five babies, holding hands,
learning how to walk.

What do *we* do?

Tickle tummies, dry up tears,

Whisper secrets in their ears, then…

Bed for baby

And me too,

Bye-bye, baby. I love

You.

MORE WALKER PAPERBACKS
For You to Enjoy

Also by Catherine and Laurence Anholt

WHAT I LIKE

"Children's likes and dislikes, as seen by six children but with a universality
which makes them appealing to all… The scant, rhyming text is elegantly fleshed out by
delicate illustrations full of tiny details." *Children's Books of the Year*

0-7445-3019-9　£3.99

KIDS

"From the absurd to the ridiculous, from the real to the imaginary, from the
nasty to the charming, this is a book which touches on the important aspects of life
as experienced by the young child." *Books for Keeps*

0-7445-3011-3　£3.99

THE TWINS, TWO BY TWO

"All families will be able to relate to this super book about bedtime… An irresistible
end-of-the-day story just right for reading together." *Practical Parenting*

0-7445-3142-X　£3.99

**Walker Paperbacks are available from most booksellers, or by post from
Walker Books Ltd, PO Box 11, Falmouth, Cornwall TR10 9EN.**

To order, send: Title, author, ISBN number and price for each book ordered, your full name and address,
cheque or postal order for the total amount, plus postage and packing:

UK and BFPO Customers – £1.00 for first book, plus 50p for the second book and plus 30p for each additional book to a maximum charge of £3.00.
Overseas and Eire Customers – £2.00 for first book, plus £1.00 for the second book and plus 50p per copy for each additional book.
Prices are correct at time of going to press, but are subject to change without notice.